THE DINOSAUR THAT POOPED A PRINCESS!

Check out Danny and Dinosaur in more adventures:

PICTURE BOOKS:

The Dinosaur that Pooped Christmas
The Dinosaur that Pooped a Planet!
The Dinosaur that Pooped the Past!
The Dinosaur that Pooped the Bed!

AND FOR YOUNGER READERS:

The Dinosaur that Pooped Daddy!
The Dinosaur that Pooped a Rainbow!

For Lola – T.F. & D.P.
For Kyle and Codie – G.P.

RED FOX

UK | USA | Canada | Ireland | Australia
India | New Zealand | South Africa

Red Fox is part of the Penguin Random House group of companies
whose addresses can be found at global.penguinrandomhouse.com.

www.penguin.co.uk   www.puffin.co.uk   www.ladybird.co.uk

Penguin
Random House
UK

First published 2018
001

Copyright © Tom Fletcher and Dougie Poynter, 2018
Illustrated by Garry Parsons
The moral right of the authors has been asserted

Printed in China

A CIP catalogue record for this book is available from the British Library

ISBN: 978–1–782–95542–9

All correspondence to:
Red Fox, Penguin Random House Children's, 80 Strand, London WC2R 0RL

THE DINOSAUR THAT POOPED A PRINCESS!

Tom Fletcher and Dougie Poynter
Illustrated by Garry Parsons

RED FOX

Once upon a time . . .

Danny was riding his dinosaur steed
    In search of a princess who longed to be freed
But soon they were lost in Fairytale Land
    So they asked for directions from Gingerbread Man.

"Gingerbread Man, Oh, Gingerbread Man,
    Show us the way we should go, if you can."

Gingerbread Man scratched his gingerbread head.
He thought for a moment then suddenly said:

"I cannot remember!
   My brain's made of dough.
But go ask the Three Little Pigs —
   They might know!"

Then as they set off down the yellow brick track
Dinosaur ate up that gingerbread snack!

They soon came across the Three Little Pigs,
    Rebuilding their houses of brick, straw and twigs.
"Three Little Pigs, Oh, Three Little Pigs,
    Princess needs help — do you know where she is?"

The Three Little Pigs made
a little pig huddle,
But they couldn't agree —
    they were all in a muddle.

"She's this way! She's that way!
    She's down there!" they said.
"Why don't you go ask
    Prince Charming instead?"

But while Danny worked out which road should be taken
The pigs smelled like bacon — so Dinosaur ate them!

They soon
found the prince
at the grand palace ball.
He made everyone laugh
– charmed the pants
off them all.

"Prince Charming, Oh,
Prince Charming, Sir,
The princess needs help
and we can't find her."

He gazed in the mirror that hung on the wall
Then the prince swooshed his hair and announced to them all:

"The path to the princess's tower is scary, And if you go forth you'll need new underweary!"

He wrote down the way they should go on a scroll . . .

Before Dinosaur swallowed that charming prince whole.

With Prince Charming's directions they started their quest . . .

Passed the troll on the bridge

and the rotten orcs' nest.

Tippy-toed
past the dragon,
asleep on
its gold,

Fooled the witch,
easy-peasy —
she was all kinds
of old!

Tamed the wolf in the wood,

Swam the sea of quicksand,

Climbed the beanstalk
and high-fived the
giant's huge hand.

But with Danny
so focused on
saving his maiden

How was he to know
that his noble steed
ate them?

"There it is! There it is!"
Danny called to his steed.
"It shan't be long now
till the princess is freed!"

"Princess, Oh, Princess,
Please let down your hair!
We've come here to save you,
But can't find the stairs!"

Danny shouted
and called
but there came
no reply . . .

So he sat on
the ground

and he started to cry.

Just then an idea pinged in Dinosaur's head:
Perhaps they could fly up the tower instead!

With fairytale creatures deep down in its gut,
Its brain made a wish involving its butt.

It knew there was only one thing it could do —
To save the princess it needed to . . .

Like a giant poo fountain they shot up the tower,
Giving Fairytale Land a smelly poo shower.

It pooped orcs and trolls
all over the place,
And the prince still looked charming
with poop on his face.

Dino's bum huffed and guffed
as he pooped out the pigs,
Blowing down their new houses
of brick, straw and twigs.

The giant, the wolf and the sea of quicksand,
The dragon, its gold and the gingerbread man.

They flew higher and higher with poop-powered thrust
And the poop was all sparkly, like brown pixie dust.

They crashed
through the roof
in a mighty
poo mess . . .

Then out of the dust came
one angry princess!

"My bedroom! It used to be pretty and blue.
And now it's all gooey and dripping with poo!
I didn't need saving — my home is this tower.
Now I'll put this mess right with my princess girl power!"

She swished with her wand
and she clicked her heels too,
And then she sang "Bibbedy,

Bobbedy,

POO!"

Loads of magic appeared from the wand in her hand . . .

And the
poop disappeared
from Fairytale Land!

"We're sorry," Dan said, "for the way we behaved.
Now we know not all princesses need to be saved!"

This story is over, the sun is descending.
But wait! There's a twist to this fairytale ending . . .

Because Dino had nothing better to do,
It swallowed the princess and pooped her out too!